the Pagemaster™

the
Pagemaster™

Adaptation by Jordan Horowitz
Based on the screenplay by
  David Kischner
  David Casci
  Ernie Contreras

From the David Kirschner
  & David Casci story

SCHOLASTIC INC.
New York Toronto London Auckland Sydney

MACAULAY CULKIN

the Pagemaster™

CHRISTOPHER LLOYD

All
The
Adventure
Your
Imagination
Can
Hold.

TWENTIETH CENTURY FOX PRESENTS IN ASSOCIATION WITH TURNER PICTURES, INC. A DAVID KIRSCHNER PRODUCTION MACAULAY CULKIN CHRISTOPHER LLOYD "THE PAGEMASTER" FEATURING THE VOICES OF WHOOPI GOLDBERG PATRICK STEWART LEONARD NIMOY FRANK WELKER ALSO STARRING ED BEGLEY, JR. MEL HARRIS MUSIC BY JAMES HORNER STORY BY DAVID KIRSCHNER DAVID CASCI SCREENPLAY BY DAVID KIRSCHNER DAVID CASCI ERNIE CONTRERAS ANIMATION CO-PRODUCERS DAVID STEINBERG AND BARRY WEISS LIVE-ACTION SCENES PRODUCED BY MICHAEL R. JOYCE PRODUCED BY DAVID KIRSCHNER AND PAUL GERTZ LIVE-ACTION DIRECTED BY JOE JOHNSTON ANIMATION DIRECTED BY MAURICE HUNT

ISBN 0-590-20244-8

™ & © 1994 by Twentieth Century Fox Film Corporation and Turner Pictures, Inc.
All rights reserved. Published by Scholastic Inc., 555 Broadway, New York, NY 10012.

12 11 10 9 8 7 6 5 4 3 2   4 5 6 7 8 9/9 0/0

Printed in the U.S.A.   40

First Scholastic printing, November 1994

PAGE ONE:
Midnight

The wind howled. WOOSH!
  Thunder exploded. BOOM!
Lightning streaked across the dark night sky.
CR-RAACK!

Richard Tyler leaped back from his window and
gasped. That lightning came awfully close, he
thought. He had once read of a man who had been
struck by lightning. The man was saved only because of the rubber soles in his shoes.

But Richard wasn't wearing any shoes. He
wasn't even wearing any slippers. He was in his
pajamas and ready for bed. His feet were completely bare.

Richard shivered with fear. His large horn-
rimmed glasses rattled on his nose. He stumbled
backwards and bumped into his desk. Then he
reached for the doorknob and scrambled out of the
room.

Richard was scared. After all, he was only ten

1

and a half years old and didn't want to get struck by lightning.

Richard ran down the hall. He hurried to his parents' bedroom. There he knew he would be safe. He was just about to knock on the door when he heard his father's voice coming from inside the room.

"Claire, how can you say that?" he heard his father, Alan Tyler, say. "Richard is *not* a normal kid."

"Alan, please," came another voice. It was Richard's mother, Claire Tyler. "Every ten year old is afraid of something."

"Yeah," replied Alan. "But every ten year old isn't afraid of *every*thing. Claire, the kid's afraid of tuna."

Mercury levels in some tuna, Richard thought to himself. He had read up on how too much could be bad for you.

"Alan," said Claire. "The world is a frightening place for Rich right now. I think we could be a little more supportive."

"Supportive?" replied Alan. "I'm the most supportive father on earth. I'm running out of supportive things to do. I signed him up for Little League. He drove the team crazy with statistics about getting hurt from being hit in the head with a ball. I agreed to coach soccer, a sport I detest, if they would please let him on the team. Did you know that getting kicked in the knee could cause shin splints in the legs? Claire, *he brought in medical evidence*. Three of my best players quit after that. So much for sports. And now I'm building him a treehouse. But he refuses to climb up to it."

"You know he hates heights," said Claire.

"I just want to be a good father." Richard heard his father sigh.

"You are a good father," Claire said reassuringly. "Maybe you're trying too hard. For now, let's just say that Richard is 'cautious' and see where it goes."

"Cautious?" Richard heard his father say with a disapproving voice. "Claire, this is way past cautious."

Richard had heard enough. He returned to his room and climbed back into his bed. He turned off his bed lamp and clicked on a flashlight.

He aimed the flashlight beam across his room and did a spot check. He saw his fire extinguisher and his complete set of disaster almanacs. He also saw his earthquake kit and his poster describing exactly what to do in case you were choking on your food. Everything was in its proper place.

Finally, he saw his special glow-in-the-dark sign over the door. It spelled *Exit* in easy-to-read green letters. It was so Richard could find his way out in case of an emergency.

As he crawled under the covers, he began to think about his dad again. Richard really didn't want to be a disappointment to him. Starting tomorrow he'd try to act more like a normal kid. But it wasn't going to be easy!

PAGE TWO:
A Dangerous Mission

The next morning Richard looked out the window. To his amazement the storm hadn't destroyed a single house on his block. Some of the other neighborhood kids were racing their bicycles down the street. They weaved daringly from the sidewalk to the street and back to the sidewalk.

Richard calculated that they were running a high risk of having an accident. He was all ready to call 911.

Richard could hear the sound of hammering in the backyard. His dad was building him a treehouse. Richard didn't want a treehouse. But he didn't want to hurt his father's feelings, either. So he thought he should act as if he liked the treehouse.

After a few more minutes Richard followed the hammering sounds out into the backyard. Pieces of lumber were scattered around a large oak tree. There was a ladder leaning against the tree and extension cables were snaked around it. In the branches of the tree sat a four-walled wooden house. It even had windows and a doorway. Alan was inside the treehouse hammering some floor-boards together. He was a handsome-looking man in his early thirties with blond hair and broad shoulders.

"Hey, Rich!" he called. He was surprised to see Richard. "Well? You like it?"

"Uh, yeah," replied Richard. "It looks great, Dad." He was trying to sound excited, but he really didn't feel that way.

"Hey, how 'bout bringing up that bag of nails?" asked Alan.

Richard grabbed a paper bag full of nails from a worktable. Then he walked over to the tree and stretched to hand the bag to his dad.

"Nah, come on up," his father prodded. "The view is terrific up here."

"I don't think so," said Richard.

"But it's solid as a rock!"

"Dad, eight percent of all household accidents involve ladders," explained Richard. "Another three percent involve trees. You're talkin' about an eleven percent probability here."

Richard took a step back, but accidentally bumped into a long piece of lumber that had been propped next to the worktable. The piece of lum-ber swung around and knocked a bucket of paint off the table. The bucket fell into a wagon. Then the wagon rolled into the ladder that was leaning against the tree. The ladder slid away from the tree, snagging an extension cord. The extension cord caught around Alan's leg and yanked him off balance. Alan came flying out of the treehouse and landed on the grassy ground below.

"You can't argue with statistics, Dad," Richard said to his father in an "I-told-you-so" tone of voice.

Just then Claire came out of the house.

"How's it goin' guys?" she asked. "Alan, your treehouse looks terrific."

"*Richard's* treehouse," said Alan insistently. He rose to his feet and brushed the dirt off his back. Then he opened his hand and presented Richard with a single nail. "Rich, you want to help?" he asked his son. "Here's something you can do. Go down to Guttman's Hardware and pick up a pound of these nails."

Richard froze.

"B-but, Dad — " he started nervously.

"No buts," Alan said firmly. "I intend to finish this treehouse before dark if it kills us."

"Us?" Richard asked, swallowing hard. He looked over at Claire. "Mom?"

Claire walked over to Richard. "Richie," she said. "Guttman's is just a short bike ride to town."

"Most traffic accidents happen within three blocks of the home," Richard reminded his mother.

"Rich, you can't base your whole life on statistics," said Alan. "You've got to take some chances." Then he stuffed a five-dollar bill into Richard's shirt pocket. "You can do this, son."

Richard realized that he had little choice. He would have to run the errand. It would be a dangerous mission.

He went into the garage. First he put on a helmet that had a special rearview mirror attached to it. Then he put on his bicycle jacket with the reflective safety tape attached to its back.

Next he checked the safety features on his bicycle. Lights, reflectors, mirrors. Fenders, horns, bells, fire extinguisher, and first aid kit. Everything was where it should be.

When he was certain that he was as prepared as he possibly could be he climbed onto his bike. He fastened his helmet tightly and slowly wheeled himself down the driveway. He looked up at the sky. Some dark clouds were forming on the horizon. He knew he would have to get to town and back before it started to rain. He looked down the street. The neighborhood kids were now taking turns jumping their bikes off a ramp.

When he felt ready Richard took a deep breath.

"Hey, look guys, it's Richard Tyler," he heard a voice call out. One of the neighborhood kids had spotted him.

Before he knew it Richard was surrounded as

the kids skidded to a stop and blocked his way.

"Get a load of his outfit," one of the kids laughed. "Where you goin', Tyler, the moon?"

"C'mon!" another kid shouted, egging Richard on. "Catch some air!"

"Go for it!" said another kid.

Richard looked over at the ramp the kids had made. It was a simple sheet of plywood propped up against a garbage can that had been laid on its side. He didn't have to do much calculating to know what the odds of an accident on that thing were. Without saying a word he turned his bike in the opposite direction and took off.

The sky overhead grew thicker with dark clouds. Thunder was beginning to rumble in the sky.

Richard began pedaling faster. He did not want to get caught in the rain. That would only increase his chances of having an accident. He saw a narrow tunnel up ahead and rode into it. The tunnel was lined with a row of dim yellow lights. One by one the lights exploded as Richard raced through.

When he came out of the other side of the tunnel the sky had become even darker. It seemed almost like the dead of night. Richard brought his bike to a stop and looked up at the sky. Suddenly a bolt of lightning streaked across the horizon. Thunderclaps exploded all around. Then thick droplets of rain began to spike Richard in the face.

Before long the drops had grown into a downpour.

Richard screamed. He wanted to turn back. He wanted to return to the safety of his room.

Then he wondered: what would be worse? His father's reaction when he returned home without the bag of nails? Or going on to Guttman's Hardware store in pouring rain?

Richard realized that no amount of calculating was necessary in this case. It was too late to turn back.

So he braced himself for the worst.

Then he began pumping his bike pedals as hard as he could.

He rode forward into the raging storm.

PAGE THREE:
The Librarian

The sidewalks were deserted as Richard turned the corner and rode into town.

The streets were becoming flooded. Richard could barely push his bicycle forward through the water. He was blinded by sheets of rain.

Suddenly a gust of wind caused a tree branch to fall directly into Richard's path. Richard swerved his bicycle out of the way. Another gust of wind caught his helmet and yanked it off his head.

Richard knew he needed shelter fast. He squinted through the sheets of pouring rain. He could make out a single, warm yellow light. It was coming from a building just down the street.

Richard steered his bicycle toward the building. It was a large brick building with white columns in the front. He skidded to a halt and ran up a long flight of stairs that led to the entrance. As he opened the door, a gust of wind pushed him forward.

Richard was out of breath and completely soaked. At least now he was safe from the raging storm outside. He looked around. The strange place seemed even bigger on the inside. The ceilings were very high. A marble staircase led to other floors. A row of statues cast huge eerie shadows across the walls.

Richard felt that he had come upon a very mysterious place.

"Welcome to the library, young man," said a deep voice excitedly

Richard jumped. The voice had come from a narrow aisle. Richard rubbed the rain from his eyes and looked down the aisle. That's when he noticed that there were many aisles. Each one held a row of shelves. And each shelf was filled with books.

There were rows upon rows of books. Shelves of books. Walls of books. Richard had never seen so many books in one place.

"I'll be right with you," came the voice again.

Richard looked down another aisle. This time he saw a tall ladder. He looked up the ladder and saw a rumpled old man standing at its top. The man returned a book to a shelf. Then the man pushed off with his foot. The ladder shot up the aisle along a thin rail. The man's wispy white hair blew back as he rode the ladder. When he reached the spot where Richard stood, he brought the ladder to a sharp and sudden stop.

"I'm Mr. Dewey, the librarian."

So that's where he was, Richard realized. *The library!*

"Don't tell me," said Mr. Dewey. His eyes were sparkling with excitement. "You're in need of a *special* book."

"M-mister," began Richard nervously. "I j-just — "

"Stop, stop, stop," said Mr. Dewey as he climbed down the ladder. "Allow me to guess. I have this talent for sensing what people need."

Mr. Dewey stuck his chest out and raised his arm in a gallant pose. "You're in need of . . . a fantasy!" he said. "Brave knights, mythical fairies, ferocious dragons, damsels in distress!"

"No, l-look," said Richard. "I need — "

"Adventure!" interrupted Mr. Dewey. He began to wave a pretend sword through the air. "Of course! You're a boy who loves adventure. You must be, to have braved nature's worst. Adventure! Brimming with wicked villains, buried treasure, and loathesome pirates who'd just as soon cut your throat as tip their hats."

"N-no," insisted Richard. "That's not what I need."

Just then, a flash of lightning flooded the tall windows. Richard gasped. The sudden shadows made Mr. Dewey look frightening.

"Horror!" exclaimed Mr. Dewey. He hunched his back and raised his arms. "That's it! Horror!

13

Wretched monsters, haunted houses, graveyards. Yes, it's horror for you, boy. I'm sure of it! Your library card, please?"

Mr. Dewey held out his hand.

"I don't have one," said Richard.

At that a light sparkled in Mr. Dewey's hand. When it was gone a library card appeared in his palm. "Now you do," said Mr. Dewey. Then he slid behind a desk and handed Richard a pen. "Sign the bottom of the card, last name first."

Richard took the pen and signed his name. Mr. Dewey took a rubber stamp and pressed it onto the card. Then he handed the card back to Richard.

"Mr. Tyler," he said, reading Richard's signature. "Consider this card your passport through the wonderful, and quite unpredictable, world of books."

"But, I'm not here for any books," said Richard finally. "That's what I've been trying to tell you. I just came in because of the storm."

"You mean you don't need — ?" Mr. Dewey began with surprise. "Oh. I see." Mr. Dewey seemed very disappointed. It was his job to make sure that all who came into the library found the books they wanted.

"Is there a phone where I can call my parents?" Richard asked the librarian.

Mr. Dewey sighed and pointed to a wall beyond the aisles of books. "Through there," he explained. "Proceed in a northeasterly direction and continue on to the rotunda. From the rotunda you will head west through the fiction section. There you will find the public telephone. You can't miss it."

Richard moved toward the aisles cautiously. There were so many rows. Suppose he made a wrong turn? Would he ever find his way back?

"Don't be afraid, boy," said Mr. Dewey. "If you lose your way merely direct yourself back to the Exit sign."

Richard looked up. A glowing green Exit sign was perched high over the entrance in front of him. It was just like the one in his bedroom.

Richard walked along the rows of books. It was like a maze. Every so often, just to be sure, he turned and glanced back at the Exit sign. As long as he could see it he knew he would be all right.

Then Richard came upon a series of aisles that were arranged like the spokes of a big wheel. Above him the ceiling gave way to a high dome. The dome was decorated with paintings of people Richard recognized as characters from famous books.

There was Captain Ahab tossing a harpoon at the giant whale from *Moby Dick*. There was the peg-legged pirate Long John Silver holding an empty treasure chest like the one he found in *Treasure Island*. There was a brave knight fighting a dragon. There was the two-faced scientist from *Dr. Jekyll and Mr. Hyde.* One side of his face was handsome, the other hideous.

In the very center of the dome was the face of a wizened old man with a long white beard and a flowing velvet robe. He seemed to be looking straight down at Richard.

"Geez," said Richard with awe. He took a step backwards. He didn't notice that some raindrops were still falling from the bottom of his coat. They had formed a small puddle around his shoes.

THUMP! Richard slipped in the puddle and hit his head on the cold marble floor of the library.

Suddenly everything went dark.

PAGE FOUR:
The Pagemaster

*D*rip, *drip, drip.* Richard felt something wet splash beside him. He reached over and touched the drops with his fingers. Each finger was covered with a different color drop.

Suddenly a blast of lightning lit the room. Richard looked up at the ceiling and gasped in horror. The painted characters had begun to melt. Colored paint was raining all about him and turning everything it touched into a painted backdrop.

Richard screamed and did his best to dodge the liquid. Before he knew it, though, he was completely splattered with color. No longer was he a human boy of bones and flesh. He had become just like the characters from the ceiling.

"I'm a cartoon!" Richard exclaimed with astonishment.

"You are an *illustration,*" came a voice from the shadows.

Richard wheeled around. A robed figure

stepped out of the shadows. He, too, was an illustration.

"W-who are you?" asked Richard with a gulp.

"I am the Pagemaster," said the man. "Keeper of the books and guardian of the written word."

The Pagemaster looked familiar to Richard.

"You're the guy from up there!" he exclaimed and pointed to the now empty ceiling. "Where're the others?"

The Pagemaster pointed to the rows of books in the room. "Why, they're here, of course," he said with a grand gesture. "And all around."

Richard was scared. He looked back the way he had come and tried to see the Exit sign, but it wasn't there.

"M-maybe you could show me the way out?" he asked the Pagemaster.

"If that is what you truly want," answered the Pagemaster.

Richard nodded.

"Splendid!" exclaimed the Pagemaster. He seemed very pleased. "Follow me."

The Pagemaster led Richard toward the book stacks.

"Is that the way?" asked Richard.

"Oh," replied the Pagemaster. "It is the *only* way."

There was a sign posted above the book stacks.

"Fiction *azz*?" Richard read, confused.

"Fiction A to Z!" corrected the Pagemaster.

"Where all is possible. Where a boy's imagination can take root and grow to incredible heights. Where a boy's fear is sometimes the road that leads to his own confidence. Where's a boy's courage is the wind that moves him to discovery. And where your journey is about to begin!"

Then, with a grand gesture the Pagemaster magically produced a book page in his hand. He flicked the page upward. As it rose to the ceiling Richard heard the thunderous sound of a giant's footsteps.

The Pagemaster produced another page. He sent this one sailing down the aisle. Suddenly, Richard heard the sound of a horse galloping.

Then to illustrate his point further the Pagemaster flung yet another page down the aisle. A strong wind began to blow. Richard heard the sound of a pounding drum. A huge Viking ship came sailing straight toward him. He quickly ducked behind the Pagemaster for safety.

Finally, the Pagemaster raised his staff. A book cart that had been sitting against the wall came to life. It scooped Richard up on its top. Richard screamed.

"Godspeed to you, boy!" shouted the Pagemaster as the book cart turned and carried Richard down the aisles at a dizzying speed. "And remember this: when in doubt, look to the books!"

They were the last words that Richard could hear the Pagemaster say. For by now he was being carried deeper and deeper into the library, speeding faster and faster between the book-shelves. All around him he heard voices coming from the books. "Once upon a time . . ." he heard a voice say. "Long ago and far away . . ." came another voice. "All for one and one for all . . ." said another.

Up ahead Richard could see a wooden telephone booth. BAM! The book cart slammed into the booth, spilling Richard on top of a pile of books.

Suddenly the books beneath him began to quiver and shake. Richard looked down just as a six-inch saber lashed up between the books. He screamed and leaped back.

"Where's the son of a rum puncheon that knocked the wind from me sails," came a voice from beneath the pile of books. "Where's he be? Where's he be?"

Then something pushed up from under the pile of books. Richard was amazed. It was an old book of adventure stories. In one hand it held the saber. Its other hand was nothing but a metal hook. It had a peg for a leg, a bandanna, and an eyepatch over one of its eyes. It was a book that looked like a pirate!

"Arrrrr!" roared the book as it slashed its saber at Richard. "So here be the lubber 'at scuffed me covers and with no apologies, too. You fiction or nonfiction?"

"I'm R-R-R-Richard," Richard answered nervously. "R-Richard Tyler."

The book scratched its top corner. "What kind of book would that be?" he asked.

"I'm not a book," replied Richard.

"Got any proof?"

Richard didn't know how to go about proving that he was a boy and not a book. He reached into his pocket and pulled out his library card. At least that would have his signature on it.

The book snatched the library card away from Richard. "A library card!" he said reading apologetically. "Beggin' yer pardon, lad. Didn't know ye was a customer. Allow me to introduce myself. They call me Adventure!"

"Look," said Richard. "I just want to get out of here."

"Of course ya do, matey," said Adventure. "We all do!"

"J-just stay away from me," Richard cried.

With that he did an about face and stepped right through a hole in the library floor!

PAGE FIVE:
Adventure

Richard plummeted downward through the hole.

"EEEOOOWWW!" Richard screamed as he tumbled down into a deep, dark pit with a pool of black water at the bottom.

Just in time a ship's anchor and chain swung in and caught him. Richard held the chain tightly as he looked down. Below him the water stirred. Then an alligator leaped up and tried to take a bite out of Richard.

Richard felt a tug from the top of the chain. He looked up and saw Adventure pulling on it. Soon Richard felt himself slowly being lifted out of the hole and back onto the library floor.

"This is a library, mate," warned Adventure. "Not everything's as it seems."

"This place is *dangerous*," said Richard breathlessly. "You said you knew the way out?"

"I know these waters like the back o' me hand,"

replied Adventure, holding up his metal hook to prove it.

"Okay," said Richard. "Let's just go!"

"Sure, mate," said Adventure. "I'd be happy t' navigate ye outta here. But there is one small favor I might be askin' in return."

"What is it?"

"Well," began Adventure. "I'm afeared I've been dry-docked in this library far longer than I'd like t' remember. Need t' breathe the open air, feel a fair wind against me pages and the good earth beneath me, er . . . foot. As I sees it, you an' yer library card are me ticket outta here. Is it a deal, mate?"

"Sure," agreed Richard anxiously. He was willing to do anything to find the exit. And he really didn't mind checking out the book.

Adventure spun around on his peg leg. "That's the spirit, lad!" he exclaimed happily. "Once we're outta here you an' me'll have many fine adventures. We'll search for buried treasure on lush green tropical islands, whar warm breezes blow — "

"I have allergies," interrupted Richard.

"Exotic ports with dirty double-crossin' scoundrels," continued Adventure. "And more fightin' than ye could ever ask fer!"

"Fighting?" Richard cringed.

"You'll never have to comb yer hair or brush yer teeth again!" promised Adventure.

"But that's unsanitary," Richard reminded him.

"Sounds too good to be true, don't it?"

"The exit?" asked Richard impatiently. "Can we get going now?"

"Aye-aye," agreed Adventure. He pointed to a ladder that was leaning against a wall of bookshelves. "First let's scale this mast and get our bearings."

"Mast?" asked Richard. "That's a ladder. I kind of have this thing about heights," he gulped.

Adventure squinted his unpatched eye at Richard. Then he reached over and pulled out a book from a shelf. It was *20,000 Leagues Under the Sea* by Jules Verne. Adventure opened the book to the chapter entitled "The Squid" and threw the book to the floor. Suddenly a huge tentacled squid popped out of the book. Richard screamed with fear and scurried to the very top of the ladder where Adventure was waiting.

"What'd you do that for?" cried Richard fearfully. "You're supposed to be helping me!"

"I *am* helpin' ya," insisted Adventure. "I'm helpin' ya find the exit."

And with that Adventure reached down and pulled his peg leg off at the knee. Then he extended it to three times its length and held it up to his eye. His peg leg was now a telescope.

Clinging tightly to the ladder Richard slowly raised up to look over the top of the bookcases. He was scared. Suddenly a foghorn sounded in the distance. He squinted hard. Between the aisles of books Richard could see some misty images take shape. Far in the distance was a mysterious island shrouded in fog. In the center of the island was a smoldering volcano.

Richard could hardly believe his eyes. Before him the greatest stories of all time had come to life. Amazing sights and sounds were coming from every direction.

All at once a bolt of lightning caught Richard's attention. Beyond it he saw a tall gabled tower with bats flying in and out of its windows. Richard ducked as the bats swooped low around his head and then flapped off into the distance.

He saw a mountain rising up from the island. The mountain was engulfed in low, misty clouds. And through the clouds Richard could just make out a dim green light.

Richard snatched Adventure's eyeglass and focused it on the green light. It was the Exit sign.

"Look!" exclaimed Richard. "Look! There it is! I see the way out!"

Just then the ladder began to shake. Adventure and Richard looked down to see what was happening. The giant squid was climbing toward them.

"Jump, boy!" Adventure cried, thinking fast. "It's jump er yer life!"

Adventure leaped off of the ladder and grabbed the opposite bookshelf with his hook.

Richard was frozen in fear. But just then the squid wrapped its tentacles around the rung of the ladder near his foot. It yanked the ladder away from the shelf and Richard found himself soaring, face first, into a wall of books.

Richard scrambled to catch hold of something so he wouldn't fall to the ground. Panicking, he grabbed the edge of a book entitled *Fantasy*. But the book slipped off the shelf and both Richard and the book plummeted toward the ground!

PAGE SIX:
Fantasy

Richard closed his eyes and braced himself for the impact. But suddenly he felt himself slowly being lowered to the ground.

Richard opened his eyes. The book he was holding had sprouted wings. And it looked very cross.

"What do you think you're doing grabbing me like that?" asked the book.

"W-well, I just — " Richard stuttered, embarrassed. "Who are you?"

"I'm Fantasy," replied the book. She waved a magic wand and curtsied. Then she noticed that Richard's library card had fallen on the floor.

"What have we here?" she asked, stepping on the card so Richard couldn't pick it up.

"It's a library card," answered Richard.

"I'm a book, honey," Fantasy snapped back. "I can read. Why, I haven't seen one of these in a while." Then she handed the card back to Richard. "Tell me, kid. What's the one thing you wish for more than anything else in the world?"

"Anything in the world?" asked Richard. "Well, right now I'd settle for just getting out of here."

"I'll grant you your wish, child," Fantasy said, raising her wand. "But you must do me one small kindness in return. *You gotta check me outta here!*"

"That's it?" Richard asked brightly. "Okay! Let's go! Should I click my heels or something?"

From his spot on the bookcase high above them Adventure didn't like what he was hearing. "Hold on there, sister," he shouted. "The lad's with me!"

"You know that short story?" Fantasy asked Richard.

"Yeah," said Richard. "He's Adventure."

"That's what they *all* say," quipped Fantasy.

"I heard that!" yelled Adventure. "I'll have ye know I'm a classic!"

"A classic misprint," said Fantasy with a sneer.

"Why, you old sea hag," Adventure said angrily. "I'll rip out yer pages and use 'em fer — "

But before he could finish he teetered and fell, screaming "Mateeey!" as he tumbled to the ground.

Richard turned to Fantasy. "Quick, do something!" he said.

Fantasy tried to save Adventure with a flick of her wand, but nothing happened. Adventure hit the ground. SPLAT!

"Oops," said Fantasy with a sheepish smile. "I

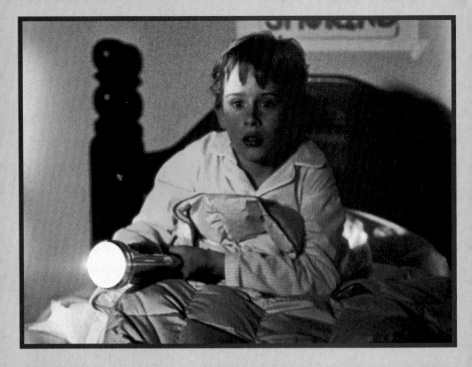

forgot. My wand only works in the fantasy section."

"You mean you *can't* wish us to the exit?" asked Richard. He was disappointed.

"I'll bet Flint's gold she's never even seen the exit," said Adventure as he stumbled to his feet and rubbed his spine.

"More than you have, shorty," said Fantasy. "In fact, the exit's just beyond my fantasy section. I see it all the time from Rapunzel's tower."

"Then what're you doin' in these parts?" asked Adventure. "There's a witches' convention 'round here, maybe?"

"I was misshelved," explained Fantasy. "But that's all over now that young Prince Charming has come to check me out." She batted her eyelashes at Richard.

Richard blushed.

"My good eye, he is," said Adventure, pulling Richard by the arm. "The lad's checkin' *me* out! C'mon, boy. It's on to the exit for us!"

Fantasy grabbed Richard's other arm and pulled him in the opposite direction. "If he thinks the exit's in that direction, it must be in this direction," she told Richard.

"Don't listen to her, mate," Adventure said as he pulled Richard back. "She's not sailin' with a full crew."

At that Fantasy fluttered her wings and a handful of sparkling fairy dust blew into Adventure's face. Adventure sneezed and fell back against a bookcase.

"Let's leave him," she told Richard. "He doesn't even know where we are now."

"Bilge water!" said Adventure. "Of course I know where we are." Adventure reached up and pulled a book down from a shelf. The book was entitled *Hound of the Baskervilles* by A. Conan Doyle. "We're in Baskervilles," said Adventure. "Have a look-see."

Adventure handed the book to Richard. Without thinking, Richard opened it. Suddenly the head of a wild hound dog lunged out with a growl. Richard screamed and tossed the book away.

Then Richard, Adventure, and Fantasy headed down the aisle as fast as they could. Behind them was the wild hound, who by now had jumped completely out of its book. It had big, sharp teeth and was growling ferociously.

Richard, Adventure, and Fantasy reached a wall that was completely lined with bookshelves. There was no place else for them to run.

Just then Richard leaned back and accidentally bumped a book off a shelf. He heard a click. The whole wall of books swung around and swept them inside to safety. Or so they thought.

All three let out a sigh of relief now that they were at least safe from that hound.

Richard noticed that they were in a new and

strange part of the library. It appeared they were standing at the entrance of a dark, eerie grave-yard. In the sky above them was a full moon shrouded by clouds. Behind them the wall was covered with thorny vines.

All at once the three heard a sound that sent shivers down their spines. It was the howl of a wolf.

And it didn't sound that far away.

PAGE SEVEN: Horror

"Are we still in the library?" asked Richard with a shudder.

"Aye, lad," whispered Adventure. "The horror section."

"It looks pretty scary," said Richard.

"That it does, mate," said Adventure. "Jest stick close to me an' ye got nothin' to worry 'bout." He didn't sound too sure.

With that Adventure pulled out his sword and cautiously led the way into the fog-covered graveyard, past some headstones. Now Richard spotted something floating in the sky. It was the exit sign.

"There it is!" Richard said, pointing excitedly. "The exit!"

But as Richard got closer he saw an old, spooky house blocking the way. The house stood at the edge of a steep cliff. Waves could be heard crashing against jagged rocks below.

"Looks like the only way to reach the exit is through that thar house," said Adventure.

Richard swallowed hard. "No way I'm goin' in there," he said.

"I'd fly you over, but I'm afraid you're too heavy," said Fantasy.

"It's yer only chance, boy," said Adventure. "It's only a house."

"Yeah, but seventeen percent of all accidents happen in or near the house," Richard warned them.

Richard, Adventure, and Fantasy slowly approached a mangled iron gate that stood in front of the house. A nameplate on the gate read: DR. JEKYLL. But beneath it someone had scratched in the name: MR. HYDE.

Richard cautiously pushed open the gate and walked up the front steps of the house. With a trembling hand he pulled the doorbell rope.

CLANG! CLANG! CLANG!

Suddenly a shadowy, horribly disfigured book fell from above the bell tower and crashed onto the ground.

Richard, Adventure, and Fantasy leaped backwards with a scream.

The strangely shaped book screamed, too. Terrified, it scrambled and climbed back up the rope.

"Come on down, ya dog-eared scalawag," shouted Adventure, waving his sword.

"Oh, put that thing away," Fantasy told Adventure. "You're frightening him." And with that

33

she flew up after the little book. "Come out, come out, wherever you are," she sang.

The misshapen book peeked out from behind its hiding place in the bell tower above the door of the house. Across the book's cover was written the word *Horror*.

"I know why you screamed," said Horror. "It's because I'm horrible. I scared you!"

"Do I look scared?" asked Fantasy.

"You mean you're *not* scared?" asked Horror.

"Of course not," said Fantasy. "Come on down."

Horror reached out to take Fantasy's outstretched hand. Slipping, he missed and fell right past Fantasy and into Richard's arms below. *Arrgh!* Richard thrust Horror back toward Fantasy, but she didn't take him.

"You mustn't judge a book by its cover," Fantasy said to Richard.

That made Horror feel so good he smiled his crooked smile.

"All right," interrupted Adventure. He was tired of waiting. "Tea time's over. Let's start navigatin' this house." He took a step closer to the haunted house.

Suddenly Horror leaped out of Richard's arms. "No!" he warned Adventure, blocking his way. "Don't go in there! It's scary inside!"

"Ha!" laughed Adventure. "I ain't a-feared o' nothin'!"

"I'm afraid," said Horror timidly.

"Of what?" asked Richard.

Horror began to list his fears one by one on his crooked, triple-jointed fingers. "I'm afraid of the dark," he began. "And dentists, butterflies, cucumbers—"

"I know just how you feel," Richard said.

"Horror always has sad endings," the hunchbacked book explained.

"I come from a world of happy endings," said Fantasy with a warm smile. "Why don't you come with us?"

"Th-through the house? I don't know . . ." Horror said nervously.

"You can do it," said Fantasy.

Suddenly Horror began to feel a little braver. He straightened his hunched back as best he could and thrust his chest out. Then he slowly walked up to the front door of the house and turned the doorknob. The door made a creaky sound as Horror pushed it open. He and his new-found friends peered into the blackness and slowly stepped inside.

The house was as old inside as it was out. Spiders and creepy crawlers scurried from view. Out of nowhere a black raven swooped down over their heads crying "Nevermore!" as it flew off.

"He-hello?" Richard called out. "Is anybody home?"

Just then every single window and door in the house slammed shut. Richard and his friends

scrambled to get out of the house. As they strug-
gled to open the front door, the doorknob came
off in their hands and fell to the floor.

They were trapped!

They watched the doorknob as it rolled away
from them. It came to a sudden stop. A big, shadowy figure had blocked its way. The figure
stepped forward. In its hand was an oil lamp that
cast a dim yellow light.

As the figure walked toward them Richard and
his friends could see the face of a kind-looking
middle-aged gentleman in the light of the lamp.

PAGE EIGHT:
The Two-Faced Terror

"**M**ay I assist you in some way?" asked the gentleman. Suddenly Richard and his friends weren't so frightened anymore.

"Hello there, Mr. — " began Fantasy.

"*Doctor* Jekyll," said the man.

"Well, sir," Richard began to explain, "we did ring the bell . . ."

"It's all my fault," explained Horror. "I was trying to help them find their way to the other side of the house."

"The other side?" asked Dr. Jekyll. Richard nodded. Dr. Jekyll placed his arm around Richard and led him deeper into the house. "My boy," he said, "I derive no pleasure in telling you that you are in extreme danger."

"Danger?" asked Richard.

"Even as we speak, lurking in this room," continued Dr. Jekyll, "are forces of evil."

"Evil?" Richard asked. By this time his knees were shaking.

Dr. Jekyll led Richard past a broken mirror and beyond a musty staircase. Then they came upon a laboratory table filled with test tubes and flasks of bubbling potions.

"Every man is possessed of both good and evil," explained Dr. Jekyll. "But enough of that. Anyone care for a drink?"

And with that Dr. Jekyll poured a test tube of bubbling potion into a wine glass. Then he gulped it down in a single swallow.

A second later Dr. Jekyll let out a loud, blood-curdling scream. He clutched his throat in pain. He threw his glass on the floor and the remaining potion spilled out. It was so powerful it burned a large hole right through the wooden planks of the floor. Dr. Jekyll stumbled and grabbed Richard for support.

Richard tried to break free, but Dr. Jekyll's grip was too strong. Now Dr. Jekyll's hands were beginning to change. They were growing bigger and hairier.

"Dr. Jekyll?" said Fantasy with concern.

Dr. Jekyll let go of Richard. Then he turned around. Fantasy gulped. Dr. Jekyll's face had also changed. His nice white teeth had become long, yellow fangs. His skin had turned gray. His eyes had turned a fiery red.

"The name," he said in a deep, raspy voice, "is Mr. Hyde!"

Suddenly Mr. Hyde took a swipe at them with

his cane. Everyone was terrified. Horror leaped to the top of a hanging chandelier for safety. But his weight caused the chandelier to pull off the ceiling and crash toward Mr. Hyde. Mr. Hyde swiped at Horror, but stumbled backwards and plummeted through the hole that had been burned in the floor, dragging the chandelier and Horror along with him.

"The stairs, mateys!" Adventure shouted. It was their only chance to escape.

"Help, Master!" called Horror. "Don't leave me!"

Horror was trapped in the chandelier. The chandelier was being pulled deeper and deeper into the hole by Mr. Hyde, who was dangling at the end of its chain.

"You've got to help Horror," Fantasy said to Richard.

But Richard was too scared to move. So Fantasy flew over to Horror and using her wand like a crowbar, untangled him from the chandelier.

Richard felt ashamed. When his friend was in trouble, he was too scared to help. Horror, however, ran up to him and grabbed his hand.

"It's okay, Master," Horror said in a forgiving voice. "If it were me I'da' been *twice* as scared!"

Richard followed his friends up the flight of stairs. All around him were sounds of clanking chains, moanings, and wailings.

"What's going on?" asked Richard breathlessly.

"Ghost stories!" explained Horror.

They finally reached a landing with four doors on it. Adventure yanked open one of the doors. A huge axe swung down and nearly sliced him in two.

Fantasy opened another door. This time a huge hairy green hand reached out and tried to grab her.

Horror opened the next door and, screaming, he quickly slammed it shut again.

"What was it?" asked Richard.

"It's dark in there," shivered Horror.

"Get in there!" said Adventure. He was anxious to find a way out and that room seemed the least dangerous. He pushed Horror through the door.

Inside was a laboratory. In the middle of the room stood a table covered with a long white sheet. All around it huge electrical machines buzzed underneath a skylight in the ceiling.

"Up there!" said Fantasy. She pointed to a staircase that led to a trap door in the skylight.

Everyone started toward the staircase, passing the sheet-covered table as they went. Suddenly a huge green hand slipped out from under the sheet and pulled it aside. Underneath was a giant with green skin that had been stitched together.

It was Frankenstein's monster. And he wasn't in a very good mood at all.

"Aaaarrrrggghhhh!" groaned the monster.

Everybody screamed and ran for the stairs. But

the monster got there first and grabbed Richard. Richard tried to save himself by hanging on to a rope.

Adventure saw that the rope was attached to the skylight. He had an idea. He quickly began to hack at it with his sword. Horror and Fantasy held on to the rope as well.

Finally the rope snapped, pulling Richard free of the monster and hurtling him, with his three friends, up through the trapdoor of the skylight.

One by one Richard and his friends landed on an observation tower on the roof of the house. Then Fantasy closed and bolted the door behind them.

"This way, mateys!" said Adventure as he leaped onto the outer wall of the deck.

Richard looked over the wall. Waves crashed in the darkness below them.

"Down there?" asked Richard. "I can't!"

"Come on, boy!" prodded Adventure. "Even books have spines!"

And with that Adventure began climbing down the side of the tower.

BOOM! BOOM! BOOM! Suddenly a pounding came from behind the skylight door. CRACK! The door burst open and the monster crashed its way through.

Fantasy pulled a torch down from its holder and created a wall of fire in front of the monster. Hating fire, the monster cringed. Then Fantasy and

Horror scurried over the wall and joined Adventure on a ledge below.

"Move it!" Fantasy called up to Richard.

"Come, Master!" shouted Horror.

Richard looked over the side of the tower. His friends seemed safe on the ledge, but the ledge looked so far away.

Behind him, the monster roared and was trying to push through the wall of flames.

Richard swallowed hard. He knew what he had to do.

PAGE NINE:
The Land of Adventure

I can do this, Richard said to himself. He climbed up and stood on top of the wall. Suddenly the stones where he stood crumbled under his feet. Richard fell screaming.

"The vine, boy!" Adventure called up. "Grab the vine!"

Richard now noticed that there were vines hanging over the side of the wall. He grabbed one. And started to climb down. All of a sudden the vine snapped and Richard fell.

THUMP! He landed on the ledge right next to his friends. Richard was surprised to find he wasn't hurt at all. "Wow!" he exclaimed. He had made it by himself.

Just then Adventure took a deep breath. "Do ye smell it?" he asked. "Breathe it in, mateys."

Everyone looked up. The Exit sign was hanging in the distance over the horizon.

Suddenly the dark sky turned bright. The sun

rose over a shimmering ocean. The sun was so bright it caused the Exit sign to disappear.

"The land of Adventure!" said Adventure. He was pointing out toward the sea.

Adventure bounded down the side of the ledge to the rocks below. Horror, Fantasy, and Richard followed right behind. Waves were crashing on the beach where he stood.

A small boat was anchored next to the rocks. Adventure jumped in and then told everyone to climb aboard. Richard eyed the boat suspiciously.

"Is it safe?" he asked. It didn't look too sturdy, he thought to himself.

"I've set to sea in worse," said Adventure. Then the book stomped his peg leg into the boat. It splintered right through the bottom and water gushed through the gaping hole.

"I'm impressed," said Fantasy sarcastically.

Now, thinking fast, Richard pulled a handkerchief out of his pocket and stuffed it into the hole. The water stopped gushing.

"Shove off, lads," Adventure ordered.

And with that Richard and Horror each took an oar and began to row.

No sooner had they taken off across the ocean than a wind began to blow. The water became choppy and uneven. The little boat rose and fell with each wave.

Four other small boats appeared. Each one was filled with rough-looking men. Standing at the bow of the first boat was a man who had a peg leg just like Adventure's!

"It's Captain Ahab, it is," said Adventure.

"Did you see it?" Captain Ahab called out from his boat.

"See what?" asked Richard.

"The devil of the deep," Adventure explained. "The white whale Moby Dick!"

"Thar she blows!" shouted Captain Ahab. He was pointing out to sea.

Everybody turned to look. Sure enough, just ahead of them, a great white whale pushed up from beneath the waves. It was Moby Dick.

Captain Ahab steered his boat toward the huge whale.

"I grin at thee, thou grinning whale!" he shouted with a crazed laugh. Then he grabbed a harpoon and flung it at Moby Dick.

That made Moby Dick terribly angry. The great white whale shot up out of the water, splintering Captain Ahab's boat in a thousand pieces.

"He's coming for *us* now!" cried Richard.

Moby Dick dove back into the ocean. For a moment all was quiet. Then, all of a sudden, the whale exploded up through the water again. This time its jaws were open wide.

"Row!" shouted Adventure. "Row fer yer lives!"

Horror and Richard began to row frantically. Moby Dick caught their boat between its huge teeth and chomped down. The boat broke in two.

Richard hit the water and sank into the ocean. Quickly, he grabbed hold of an empty barrel that had been knocked out of the boat. He and the barrel rose up to the ocean's surface.

Richard gasped for air. Then he looked around. There was nothing to be seen, except the splintery remains of his boat.

But where were his friends?

"Guys?" he called out weakly. "Where are you?"

No one answered. Richard was all alone in the middle of the vast blue sea.

Suddenly the water around Richard began to stir. Richard grew frightened and dogpaddled over to a raftlike plank. He grabbed onto the wooden plank and climbed aboard.

Then something popped out of the water and grabbed the plank as well. It was Adventure.

"Adventure!" said Richard with glee. "Boy, am I ever glad to see you."

Richard hugged Adventure tightly. But all Adventure could do was sputter and cough.

"Where're Horror and Fantasy?" asked Richard.

"I searched for 'em as much as I could, mate," said Adventure once he had caught his breath. His voice was filled with sadness. " 'Fraid they've gone down below with Davy Jones."

"No!" exclaimed Richard. He didn't want to believe that his friends were gone forever. "Horror!" he called out to the sea. "Fantasy!"

Richard called out in all directions. Suddenly his eyes went wide. Heading right for them was a bunch of hungry-looking sharks!

The sharks surrounded Richard and Adventure. They snapped their razor-sharp teeth at them. Richard and Adventure shook with fear.

Just then a boat appeared in the distance.

"Help!" Richard shouted to the boat. "Over here!"

The boat turned and headed toward Richard and Adventure. Once it reached them a group of scruffy-looking sailors helped them aboard and to safety. They all were unshaven and filthy. Many were missing most of their teeth. And each one had a gun tucked into his belt.

Adventure didn't trust them at all.

"It's a good thing you guys came along," said Richard. "We're missing two others. Have you seen them?"

One of the sailors spit. "Ye's all the catch we had t'day," he said in a menacing voice.

As he said this another boat pulled up beside them. It was ten times as big as the smaller one. Its huge sails blew in the wind. A flag flew at the top of its mast. The flag had a picture of a skull and crossbones on it.

It was the Jolly Roger. The ship was a pirate ship!

PAGE TEN:
Buried Treasure

The next thing they knew Richard and Adventure were tossed roughly onto the deck of the pirate ship. All around them were mangy, laughing pirates. One of them pulled out a knife and pointed it at Richard. Another raised his sword to Richard's throat.

"Give the word, Cap'n Silver, sir," said the pirate with the knife, "and I'll show ye the color of his insides."

"Stow yer cutlass, Tom Morgan," a voice bellowed. "I want a better look at his outsides first!"

Richard looked up, his knees shivering with fear. The biggest pirate on the deck limped over on his peg leg. Richard knew who he was. He had read about him in the book *Treasure Island*.

"Long John Silver?" asked Richard in astonishment.

"Aye, lad," said John Silver. "The very same."
John Silver looked Richard up and down.

"Well, seein' as how me men plucked ye out of the water like a drownin' bilge rat," he said. "you'll be joinin' our happy family as our new cabin boy."

"Uh, thanks," said Richard apologetically. "But I already have a family. And I really should be getting home now."

Just then all the pirates pulled out their swords and guns and aimed them at Richard.

"I think ye *are* home," said John Silver with a grin.

Seeing his friend in danger made Adventure mad. He jumped on to the railing and pulled out his saber.

"Touch one hair on the boy's head and you'll be answering to me!" he shouted.

All the pirates laughed at Adventure. They weren't afraid of him. After all, he was only about as big as a book.

While they were talking, one of the sailors snuck up behind Adventure and pushed him onto the deck. Long John Silver bent over and picked up the feisty book by its pages.

"Well, well," Silver said to Adventure. "Ye wouldn't happen to be goin' after me treasure, would ye now?"

Adventure laughed. He already knew the ending of *Treasure Island*.

"You ain't got any treasure worth goin' after," he told Silver.

Silver's men began to murmur with concern. After all, they had signed aboard only to find treasure.

"He's lyin'," Silver said to his men. "There's plenty o' treasure for all of ye! Search 'im — and the boy, too."

The pirates grabbed Adventure and Richard by the feet and shook them upside down. Richard's library card popped out of his pocket.

"My library card!" Richard exclaimed, grabbing for the card.

But Silver snatched it away. "A cabin boy don't need no library card," he said. And with that he threw the card into the ocean.

Richard and Adventure watched the card disappear, along with their only hope of getting out of the library.

"Land ho!" one of the pirates shouted.

Everybody rushed to the other side of the ship and looked out toward the horizon. Not far away was an island with a rocky point in the shape of a skull.

"There she be, mateys," said Silver. "Treasure Island!"

All the pirates let out a cheer. Then they rushed to their posts and began to steer the ship in the direction of the island.

Once on shore the pirates eagerly climbed onto the beach. Tom Morgan unfolded a map, but nobody was sure how to read it. Then one of the pirates saw some skeleton bones laid out on the sand. The bones were pointing to a tree directly ahead of them.

"What sort of way is that for bones t'lie?" asked one of the pirates. "T'ain't natural."

"This island's haunted," said Tom Morgan. "It's accursed, it is."

"Ah, yer all yellow dogs," bellowed John Silver. "Open yer eyes. The bones is a compass pointin' t'way to the treasure!"

All at once the pirates charged toward the tree. When they got there they let out a sigh of disappointment.

Someone had dug a big hole where the treasure should have been. In the hole sat a huge treasure chest, but it was completely empty.

"It's gone!" exclaimed Tom Morgan.

One of the other pirates scrambled about the ditch. He found a single gold coin.

"This is your treasure, is it?" the pirate said, showing the coin to John Silver.

"Stand by for trouble," Adventure whispered to Richard.

"We mighta known you'd double-cross us," said another pirate.

John Silver went for his gun, but the other pirates beat him to the draw.

"Throw down yer weapons, John Silver," said one of the pirates.

"You'll regret this," said John Silver.

"Save yer speeches," said the pirate. "Dead men don't bite." And with that all the pirates took aim at their captain and prepared to fire.

Richard swallowed. Adventure shut his eye.

Just then a horrifying moan came from up above. It sounded like a ghost. The pirates became frightened.

"Evil spirits!" exclaimed Tom Morgan.

Suddenly something dropped from the branches of a tree.

It was Horror!

"Horror!" exclaimed Richard with surprise. "You're alive!"

"Not for long!" said one of the pirates. The pirate raised his musket and aimed it at Horror. But just as the pirate was ready to fire he was hit in the face with a blast of fairy dust.

The pirate sneezed as he pulled the trigger. The shot exploded upward, hitting some coconuts in a tree. The coconuts fell and knocked the pirates out cold.

"Fantasy!" said Richard, looking up. Indeed, Fantasy was alive and well, fairy dust and all.

"At your service," she said with a polite curtsy.

Richard noticed that Long John Silver was standing right across from him. His eye was on a sword that lay on the ground.

"The sword, kid," Fantasy whispered to Richard. "Get the sword."

"Don't even think of it, boy!" warned John Silver. "Ye ain't got the heart!"

Richard eyed the sword and gulped. John Silver was inching his way toward it. Richard knew he had to get the weapon first or he and his friends would never make it to the exit.

That's when Richard closed his eyes and made a jump for the sword.

PAGE ELEVEN:
True Friends

Richard opened his eyes. Much to his surprise Long John Silver was standing over him, empty-handed. That was because Richard had gotten hold of the sword first.

"Stay back!" Richard commanded. His trembling hand pointed the sword at the pirate captain.

"Avast there, laddie," said John Silver. "Somebody could get hurt with that blade ye got there."

"I know," said Richard. "Twenty-three percent of all injuries are caused by knives or other sharp objects."

John Silver had no idea what Richard was talking about.

"You're not gonna make me get on that thar ship and sail away, are ye?" he asked Richard.

"I'm not?" asked Richard nervously. Then he thought better. "I mean, I am! That's exactly what I'm gonna do."

Long John Silver could tell that Richard meant

business. He backed himself down the beach and climbed into one of the small boats.

"Ye be a hard lad, Richard Tyler," said the captain as he shoved off. "Good sailin' to ye, shipmate."

And with that Long John Silver rowed himself back to his ship and sailed away to sea.

Horror and Fantasy cheered as soon as the pirate had gone.

"Wow!" Richard said with relief. "I wish my Dad coulda seen me! And I thought you two were goners!"

"We almost were," said Fantasy, slipping her arm through Horror's. "That is, until this enchanting fellow discovered he could float."

Horror knocked on his hump. "It's hollow," he explained.

THUMP! THUMP! THUMP! Suddenly everyone heard a loud pounding. It was coming from the treasure chest.

"Who's there?" Horror asked the chest.

"Adventure!" came a voice from inside.

"Adventure who?" called Horror, jumping on the chest.

"Whaddaya mean, 'Adventure who?' " yelled Adventure. "Lemme outta here you dog-eared — "

Horror opened the trunk and Adventure popped out. He had been accidentally trapped inside during the fight with the pirates.

"I was just thanking these guys for saving us," Richard told Adventure.

Adventure wrinkled his brow. "I coulda taken the lot of 'em with one hand tied behind me back!" he grumbled. Then he wheeled around and stomped off in a huff.

"That's just his way of saying thanks," Richard explained to Horror and Fantasy.

Horror ran after Adventure. Along the way he picked up a bandanna from one of the unconscious pirates and wrapped it around his head.

"Ahoy, matey!" Horror called to Adventure. He was trying his best to look and sound just like Adventure. "Aye, we're brave, adventurous men."

But Adventure was still angry. "Go away," he told the hunchback. "Ye don't know what yer talkin' about."

"I know I'm not your favorite kind of book," said Horror. "But I could be just like you."

Adventure laughed at Horror. "You'll never be Adventure," he said. "You ain't got the spine fer it."

With that Adventure stomped off down the beach, grumbling to himself all the way. Horror felt sad as he watched Adventure walk away. He wanted to be friends with Adventure. He wished he could be more like Adventure, too. Adventure was brave and courageous while Horror was scared of even the sound of a pin dropping.

Adventure had walked only a few yards down the beach when a piece of paper blew up on shore and became stuck to his peg leg. He tried to shake it off, but it was stuck tight. So he reached down and peeled it off with his hook.

A wide smile came over his face when he saw what the piece of paper was. He wheeled around and clomped hurriedly back to Richard and Fantasy.

"Pick one," said Adventure. He was holding out his clenched hand and his hook.

Richard pretended to think for a minute. Then he picked Adventure's hand. Adventure opened his fingers. The piece of paper was sitting in his palm.

Richard recognized the piece of paper instantly. "My library card!" he exclaimed with glee.

"Library card?" asked Fantasy.

"Wrestled it away from three sharks who was eyein' it fer breakfast," fibbed Adventure. "At no small threat to me life, neither."

Richard looked around. "Where's Horror?" he asked. "Wasn't he with you?"

"He was," said Adventure. "But he — I mean I sort of — he kinda — "

"What did you say to him now?" asked Fantasy. She knew that Horror was very sensitive.

"Well, I — uh — " Adventure said with embarrassment. "I'll go find him." Then he turned around and ran back down the beach.

"Horror!" Adventure called. "Horror! Where are you?"

Adventure heard a commotion coming from behind a sand dune. He quickly climbed to the top of the dune. Down below he saw that Horror was being tied to the ground by an army of six-inch-high people. Adventure recognized the people as Lilliputians. They had captured Horror just as if he were the giant from the book *Gulliver's Travels*. A series of ropes tied his lifeless looking body to the ground.

"Hang on, mate!" shouted Adventure. "I'm comin'!"

Immediately, Adventure charged over the sand dune. The Lilliputians filed into formation and let loose a flurry of arrows when they saw him.

Adventure flipped open his covers like a shield. The arrows simply bounced off him. Then he pulled out his sword and charged the Lilliputians. The army of tiny people fled in a panic. When they were out of sight Adventure untied Horror.

"Speak t'me, mate!" said Adventure. Horror seemed lifeless. Adventure lowered his head in sadness. "Ye had a good heart," he said softly. "And ye was braver than ye knew. I'd walk t'plank if I thought it would bring you back."

Just then Horror opened his eyes. "Ya would?" he asked with a big smile. Adventure's eyes widened with surprise. Horror was alive after all!

At that same moment Richard and Fantasy came climbing over the sand dune.

"Are you okay?" Richard asked Horror.

"Thanks to my friend here," said Horror. Then he gave Adventure a big hug.

"Get off me!" grumbled Adventure as he pushed Horror away. Richard and Fantasy smiled. They knew that Adventure was as happy as they were to see that Horror was all right.

But before anybody could say another word Fantasy's wand began to blink on and off.

"Did you see that?" asked Fantasy. "My wand! It's blinking! That can only mean one thing!"

"The exit!" exclaimed Richard.

"The checkout!" shouted Adventure.

"A happy ending!" clapped Horror.

Soon Fantasy's wand began to vibrate. Then, all by itself, it gently led Fantasy toward a lush tropical forest that lay just ahead.

Richard, Adventure, and Horror followed. They really weren't sure where they were going or why. They only knew they had to follow the magic wand to find out.

PAGE TWELVE:
Fantasy Land

Richard and his friends followed the wand into the forest. The forest was dark with tropical foliage. Trees hung heavy with buds. As Richard walked past, the buds unfolded, offering not flowers, but books. The ground was wet and mossy, but it made a pattern that reminded Richard of the library floor.

Soon the dark colors of the forest began to change. Many new and more brilliant colors fanned out before them. The spectacle filled Richard with awe. He pushed through a flower-lined thicket into a magical meadow. Fairy dust shimmered everywhere.

"Wow," said Richard with wonder. "Look at this place!"

In the distance Richard saw a handsome prince climbing a long yellow rope to a tower. As he got closer Richard realized that the rope was really the braided hair of the prince's true love. Her name was Rapunzel.

Glancing in another direction Richard saw a horse and carriage rush by. Suddenly the carriage transformed itself into a pumpkin. The horses became mice.

Richard was still looking at the mice when a cluster of tiny fairies surrounded him and the others. One of the fairies mischievously plucked Richard's glasses off his nose. Another took Adventure's sword. Richard and Adventure chased the fairies up a hill. The fairies split up at the entrance of a small cave. Some carried Richard's glasses up to a ledge over the cave. The others took Adventure's sword into the cave itself.

Richard climbed to the ledge above the cave and took his glasses back from the fairies. When he looked up he let out a gasp. Beyond where he was standing was a high mountain made of books. At the top of the mountain light radiated in all directions. Above the light was the Exit sign.

"Geez!" said Richard, half aloud. "There it is!"

Meanwhile, Adventure had just reached the entrance to the cave. He hesitated before going in after his sword. After all it *was* a cave. And caves *were* kind of dark.

"Whatsa' matter?" Fantasy asked him. "Is 'Adventure' afraid to go in?"

"Are you kiddin', sister?" replied Adventure. "I live for moments like this."

And with that Adventure cautiously entered the cave.

The cave was slimy and damp inside. Pointed mineral formations hung from the ceiling and rose from the ground.

Adventure saw his sword on the floor and quickly snatched it up. He was happy to have it back and slashed it through the air to make sure it was all right. In doing so he accidentally sliced off one of the formations.

Suddenly the ground began to rumble. Adventure's eyes went wide as he was nearly thrown off his feet. It was an earthquake!

Outside Richard was flung from side to side as the top of the cave shook. He grabbed hold of a thick tree trunk for safety.

All at once two huge boulders began to shake loose in front of him. But instead of rolling toward him the boulders split open from the middle. Behind them were two giant-sized glowing red eyes!

That's when Richard realized he wasn't on top of a cave at all. The eyes were those of a fierce, fire-breathing dragon. What he thought was a tree trunk was the horn on the nose of the terrible dragon. And Richard was standing on the snout of the dragon itself!

Inside the cave Adventure had come to the same conclusion himself. That wasn't a pointed rock he sliced off with his sword. It was one of the dragon's teeth! Now the dragon was really angry.

Adventure ran as fast as he could to get out of

the dragon's mouth. But a fireball was close on his heels. Adventure tripped. Just then a hand reached into the dragon's mouth and plucked Adventure to freedom.

It was Horror!

No sooner had Horror pulled Adventure free than the dragon belched and a raging flame shot out of its mouth. Horror and Adventure would have been burned to a crisp had they not made it to the ground below in time.

Meanwhile Richard was hanging on to the dragon's horn for dear life. The dragon shook its head and sent Richard hurtling through the air.

Fantasy spun around to Horror. "Quick!" she said, pointing to her pages. "Find page one thousand and one."

Horror licked his finger and flipped through Fantasy's pages until he found the one she was looking for. It was the first page of a story called *Tales From the Arabian Nights*.

Slamming her cover shut, Fantasy quickly took the page from Horror. Then she tossed it into the air and tapped it with her magic wand. The page became a flying carpet.

"Get the boy!" Fantasy commanded the carpet.

The carpet obeyed. It dipped and swirled and swooped up Richard just before he hit the ground.

"C'mon!" Richard said to the others. "The exit's up there!" he said pointing to the top of the mountain.

Everybody jumped onto the flying carpet. The carpet zoomed into the sky toward the Exit sign, with the dragon trailing not far behind.

Higher and higher the carpet soared. It passed vast cloud cities and flying camels. It even flew by Aladdin and his magic genie.

"We're gonna make it!" exclaimed Richard as the carpet approached the top of the mountain.

Horror was so excited he jumped for joy. In doing so, however, he knocked Fantasy's magic wand out of her hand. The wand fell over the edge of the carpet and down through the clouds. There the dragon was, flying upward after the carpet. The dragon quickly snapped up the wand and swallowed it.

"Oh, dear," moaned Fantasy. "I wish that hadn't happened."

Just then the dragon let out another fireball. This one hit the carpet and sent it reeling into the side of the mountain. Everybody tumbled off onto a ledge.

Richard shook the rubble out of his hair and, looking up, saw that they were very close to the top of the mountain.

And the exit.

Richard began to climb hurriedly toward the sign. As Horror, Fantasy, and Adventure started to follow, a giant shadow fell over them. Their spines began to shake.

The dragon!

Meanwhile, Richard was hurriedly making his way up the side of the mountain unaware that his friends were in danger.

"We're almost there!" he said as he moved from one ledge to another. Soon the Exit sign was within reach. "We made it! C'mon! Guys?"

That's when Richard looked down and saw that no one was following him. His friends were trapped in a crevice on the ledge below and the dragon was hovering over them. Out of its mouth came a searing burst of flame.

Horror, Fantasy, and Adventure flattened themselves against the side of the mountain. The dragon's burst of fire missed them only by inches.

Richard watched from above. He saw that his friends needed his help below. Up above him, though, was the exit and his way home. Richard could not decide which way to go.

"Help, Master!" he heard Horror call out to him.

Richard hesitated. The exit was only a few feet away. Just a few more steps and he would be free.

But he couldn't do it. They were his friends and he wasn't going to let them down this time. He spun around and started back down the mountain.

Halfway down he came upon a soldier's skeleton. He took the skeleton's sword and shield. Then he put on its helmet. Now he was ready to face the dragon.

"I'm coming!" Richard called down to his friends. He bravely ran up behind the dragon and swung at its tail with his sword.

The dragon roared, releasing a funnel of fire. Richard blocked it with his shield.

" 'At's it, boy!" shouted Adventure. "Go fer t'gizzard!"

"Watch out for its tail!" warned Fantasy.

"Bite 'im!" yelled Horror. "Bite 'im!"

Richard raised his sword and aimed for the dragon's huge stomach. But before Richard could strike, the dragon whipped its tail around and snatched Richard up. The sword and shield were shaken from Richard's hands. Then the dragon held Richard with its tail and dangled the boy in front of its face.

"Put me down, you ugly lizard!" Richard yelled angrily.

Just then the dragon smacked its lips and opened its mouth. It slowly raised Richard high into the air. With a blink of an eye it tossed Richard down its throat, swallowing him with one swift gulp.

PAGE THIRTEEN: Belly of the Beast

Richard tumbled downward and downward along the cushiony insides of the dragon's throat. Then he landed on the slimy, but soft pit of the dragon's stomach. THUMP!

All around Richard were various library items that the dragon had swallowed for one meal or another. Old bones and seashells were scattered about. There were tree branches with books for buds. There was even an old, broken book cart and many, many books.

"This must be the dragon's stomach," Richard said aloud. "I gotta get outta here."

Then Richard recognized a long, thin object glistening next to some fish bones. It was Fantasy's wand!

Richard quickly waved the wand and wished himself out of the dragon's belly. But when he looked around he saw that he hadn't moved. The wand didn't work for him. Disappointed, he slipped it into his back pocket.

Next he crawled on top of the book cart and tried to climb up out of the dragon's stomach. The sides of the dragon's throat were so slippery, though, that Richard kept sliding back down.

Suddenly he remembered the words the Pagemaster had said to him before he became lost.

" 'Look to the books,' " he repeated to himself. So he began looking at some of the books that lay around him.

The first one he grabbed was *Alice in Wonderland*. He opened it up and the Queen of Hearts popped out.

"Off with his head!" screamed the Queen of Hearts. Richard quickly snapped the book shut.

Then he found another book called *Jack and the Beanstalk*. Yeah, this is it, he thought. A beanstalk was just what he needed to climb out of the dragon's throat. He opened the book eagerly.

A giant beanstalk thrust up from the book's pages. Richard clung tightly to its branches as it lifted him higher and higher up through the dragon's throat.

Meanwhile, the dragon felt a strange tickle and opened its mouth wide. Out shot the giant beanstalk, Richard and all!

Adventure, Horror, and Fantasy were happy to see that Richard was alive. As Richard passed, all three jumped on to the rising beanstalk and joined the ride to the top of the mountain.

"Jump!" shouted Richard. "Everybody jump!"

The four of them leaped off the beanstalk and onto the mountaintop. When they were sure they were safe they sighed with relief.

"Are you all right?" Fantasy asked Richard. Richard was too dazed to answer.

"Master, you saved us," said Horror.

"That ye did, matey," added Adventure.

Richard smiled. Then he took the wand out of his back pocket and proudly handed it to Fantasy.

"My hero," said Fantasy as she kissed Richard on the cheek.

Richard pushed his glasses back up on his nose and looked upward. An ancient dome-roofed observatory stood before them. Hovering over it were the glowing green letters of the Exit sign.

One by one they entered through the great door of the observatory. In the center of the room a large crystal dome glowed with a magnificent whirlwind of white light.

Suddenly a shadow shifted across the room.

"Who's there?" asked Richard.

Slowly the mysterious figure stepped into the light. Adventure respectfully removed his bandanna. Horror stood at attention. Fantasy curtsied. Richard instantly recognized the white-bearded face and flowing robe of the figure.

It was the Pagemaster, of course.

"Hey," said Richard. "How'd *you* get here?"

"Now, now," Fantasy said to Richard in a very humble voice. "We're in the presence of the Pagemaster."

"I know who he is," said Richard. "He's the guy who did all this to me." Then he walked right up to the Pagemaster and looked him straight in the eye. "Do you have any idea what I've been through?" he asked.

"Tell me," said the Pagemaster.

"I was nearly torn apart by a madman. I was made a slave by a bunch of mangy pirates. And eaten, got that, *eaten* by a fire-breathing dragon. Not to mention being tossed, squashed, and scared practically to death!"

"Yet you stand before me," the Pagemaster pointed out.

Richard didn't know what to say. "Well . . . yeah," he finally agreed.

Horror crawled up to the Pagemaster. "He don't mean nothin' by it, my Pagemaster," he said apologetically. "He don't mean nothin'."

"Nonsense," said the Pagemaster. "The boy is right. I purposely sent him through the fiction section."

"So you admit it!" said Richard.

"Of course," the Pagemaster laughed. "Think, boy! What kind of adventure would you have had if I'd brought you here with a turn of the page."

With a wave of his hand the Pagemaster suddenly made all the characters that Richard had encountered on his search for the exit appear in the funnel of light.

"You prevailed over evil," said Dr. Jekyll.

"Ye looked Moby Dick in the eye, boy!" said Captain Ahab.

"Ye had pirate stuff, m'lad," said Long John Silver. "And don't no one speak any different."

"If I had brought you here from the start," said the Pagemaster, "you never would have found the courage to face your own fears. And in doing so, you triumph here and always."

Richard realized that the Pagemaster was right. At first he had been frightened of practically everything. Now he wasn't afraid of anything.

Adventure lifted his sword in honor of Richard.

Horror smiled his horrible smile.

Fantasy cast a halo of fairy dust over Richard's head.

The Pagemaster drew his arm over the crystal dome. Looking into the dome Richard saw the rotunda room of the library. Lying on the floor, the real-life Richard, was still out cold.

"Hey, that's me!" said Richard.

"That *was* you," said the Pagemaster. "The world awaits."

And with that Richard, Horror, Adventure, and Fantasy were swept into the swirling whirlwind of light and sucked back through it into the library below.

71

PAGE FOURTEEN:
Exit

Richard opened his eyes and realized he was back in his old body lying on the rotunda floor. Above him was the painted dome. Once again he saw the paintings of the classic characters of fiction. Dr. Jekyll and Mr. Hyde, Captain Ahab and Long John Silver stared back at him.

Right in the center was the painting of the wizened old Pagemaster.

Richard looked down at his hands. They were no longer the bright colors of a cartoon. Now they were real flesh and bone.

"You took quite a spill, young man," came a voice.

Richard looked up. Mr. Dewey was picking up three books that had fallen next to Richard. Beyond Mr. Dewey, Richard spotted the glowing green Exit sign. Jumping to his feet, he sprinted toward the sign.

Suddenly he skidded to a stop. He turned around and ran back to Mr. Dewey.

"Wait!" he told the old librarian. "I forgot something."

He quickly plucked the three books out of Mr. Dewey's arms. In their place he handed Mr. Dewey his now torn and tattered library card.

The librarian took one of the books away from Richard. "I'm afraid you can only check out two today," said Mr. Dewey.

"But I promised him," said Richard sadly.

"Promised whom?"

Richard pointed to the book Mr. Dewey had taken. It was *Horror*.

Richard realized that promising a book to take it out of the library must have sounded pretty silly.

"Look," he explained. "I need . . . I mean . . . you think just this once — ?"

Mr. Dewey smiled. He handed the book back to Richard.

"Just this once," he said.

Richard clutched the three books and ran through the doors of the library. His bicycle was sitting right where he had left it.

Richard pedaled home as fast as he could. He crossed the main avenue of town and turned down the side streets. He rode through the tunnel that led back to his neighborhood. As he turned a tree-lined corner he slowed down and came to a full stop. Dead ahead was the ramp. It was the one the neighborhood kids had challenged him to jump.

Richard's heart pounded. He steered his bike toward the ramp. Faster and faster he went, faster than he had ever gone before. He hit the ramp at full speed and the bike lifted into the air, higher than any kid had ever gone. He landed safely on the ground and pedaled on, never looking back once.

Richard rode home as fast as he could. As he parked his bike he caught sight of the treehouse his father had built for him. Somehow the treehouse didn't seem as high as it once had. It certainly wasn't as high as the top of the dragon's head. And the ladder was certainly not as tall as a beanstalk.

Exhausted from his adventure, Richard used the little energy he had left and crawled up the ladder into the treehouse. Then Richard fell asleep with his books safely tucked in his arms.

Richard was still sleeping when his parents arrived home and found him in the treehouse. They were so happy to see that he was safe that they didn't want to wake him up. So they quietly turned off the lantern and went into the house.

When they had gone one of the books stood up on its own and looked around.

"Aye, this be the land of Adventure," said the familiar voice of Adventure. "You can lay to that."

Horror rustled its pages nervously. "It's dark

out here," he said timidly. "I wish there was a nightlight."

"Honey, wish granted," said the third book whose title was Fantasy. Then she fluttered her wings and twirled her magic wand.

The lantern's light popped brightly on as fairy dust shimmered to the floor around it.